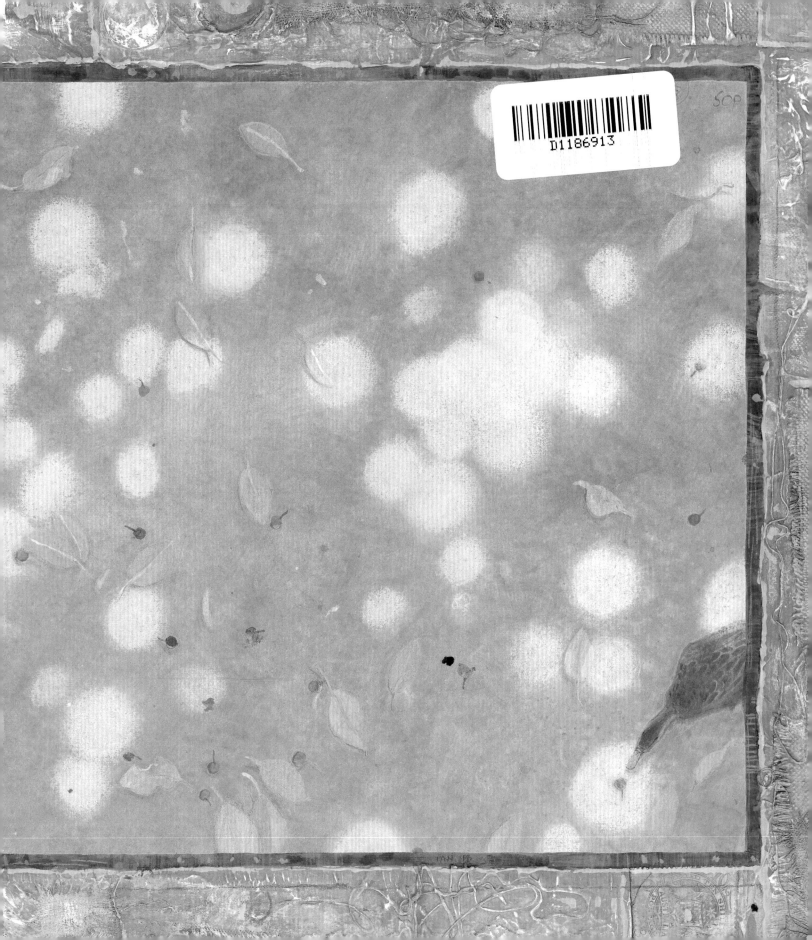

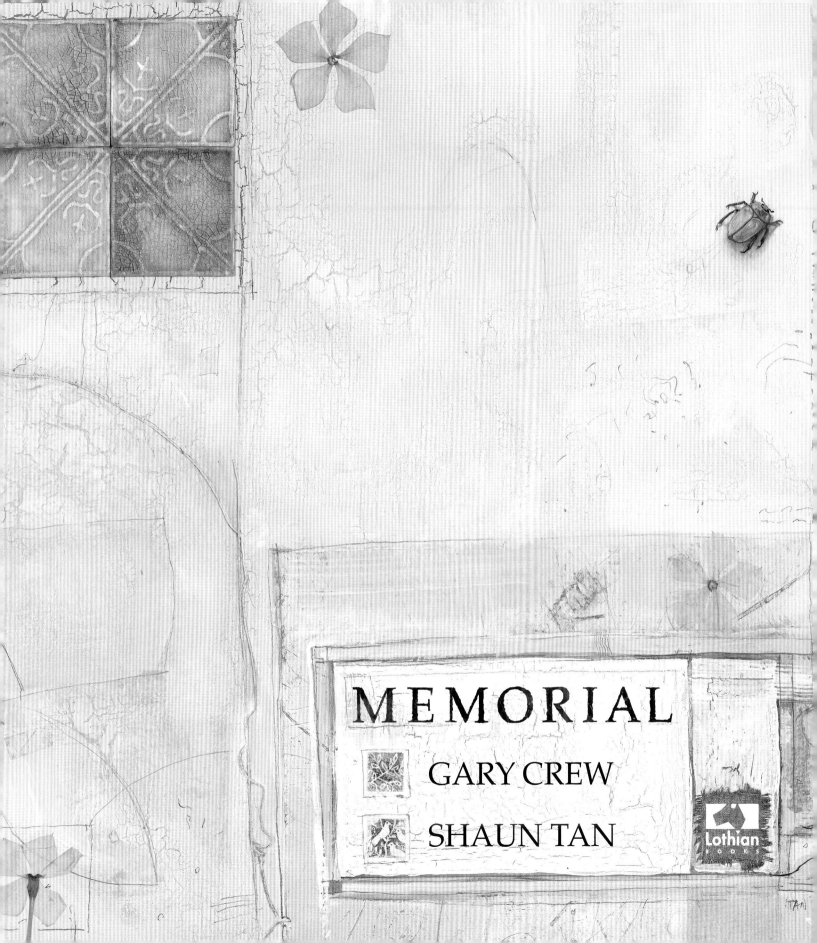

MEMORIAL

GARY CREW

SHAUN TAN

Thomas C. Lothian Pty Ltd
132 Albert Road,
South Melbourne, Victoria 3205.

National Library of Australia
Cataloguing-in-Publication data:
  Crew, Gary, 1947– .
  Memorial.

  ISBN 0 7344 0545 6.

  I. Tan, Shaun. II. Title.

A823.3

Design by Shaun Tan
Typography by Elizabeth Farlie
Colour reproduction by
  Scott Digital, Port Melbourne
Printed in Hong Kong by
  Wing King Tong

My great-grandpa says they planted the tree
on the day he came home from the war.

He says he stood at the crossroads and watched the ceremony. He was with the other town boys who had joined up — or what was left of them.

'We got chopped to bits at Ypres,' he says. 'But …' and he shrugs and he sniffs and he wipes his watery eyes and his grizzled cheeks.

'It's the sun,' he says. 'Too bright for an old fella.' Then he tells me more about the tree.

'I come home in 1918,' Old Pa says. 'There was nothin' at the crossroads then, only dirt. But that day the mayor says, "I declare this place a Shrine of Remembrance. Lest we forget."

'Then this boy scout, Issy Jacobs it was — died in the next war himself —

well, he steps up and plays the reveille.

'Next comes two nurses — young Ruby Vale and your grandma …'
'My great-grandma, Old Pa.'
'Ah,' he says. 'I reckon you remember better than me, son.'

Old Pa's funny like that. He remembers the tiny details but forgets what you might call the big picture.

'Anyway, out comes Ruby and my Betty, and they pull the sheet off the statue there …'

'The unknown soldier, Old Pa,' I say, showing off.

'I know,' he says. 'We were smart as paint in our uniforms, the five of us town boys. We took turns with the shovel until the hole was good and deep.

'Then little Philly Whipps wheeled himself over with this piddly Moreton Bay Fig tree on his lap. All done up in hessian, it was. Philly lost his legs to shrapnel. But it was my Betty, your great-grandma, who planted that tree …

'That's something I'll never forget …'

'It sure wasn't no piddly tree when I remember it,' my grandpa says. 'That was around '35, when your Old Ma starts dragging me to the barber's shop down that way. She said I looked like a hobo. But I scooted up that tree and I wouldn't come down. Geez, I put on a turn. She got me, though. She gets a hose turned on me from the tap in the park.'

Then he starts scratching his shiny bald head and looking confused. 'I wish I had all that hair now.'

'You were talking about the big town tree, Pa. The one the council wants to chop down.'
    I'm remembering that all old people forget.

'That big town tree? Well, they had the memorial service in that park when I came home too.'

'March '46,' Ma says, pouring the tea. 'When the ceremony was over we had morning tea on trestle tables all set out nice under that tree — right beside the statue of the unknown soldier.

'Even then the roots were lifting the base of the statue so it had a bit of a lean on it — not that we would have noticed that day. We used the silver tea service from the council office. Couldn't keep his hands off me, your pa couldn't.'

'Not then nor now,' Pa gives Ma a hug. 'There's a lot of special memories under that tree, Audrey. Like coming home after the pictures, eh?' and he gives her a bit of a pinch.

'Under that tree was always cool in summer,' she says. 'A good place for a breather.'

'You know your mother and I had a tree house up there?' Dad says right out of the blue. 'We used to play doctors and nurses. And mothers and fathers, didn't we …?'

Mum looks a bit worried. Dad can come out with anything sometimes. 'You and your mothers and fathers,' she says, biffing him. 'And you were always trying to get me up there to look at the stars — or so you said. But the kids don't play there any more. There's not even any grass. The park's all covered with bitumen now. Last time I remember seeing grass there was in '72 — at the memorial service when you came back from Vietnam.'

'Were you in Vietnam, Dad?'

'There's some things you don't want to remember, son …'

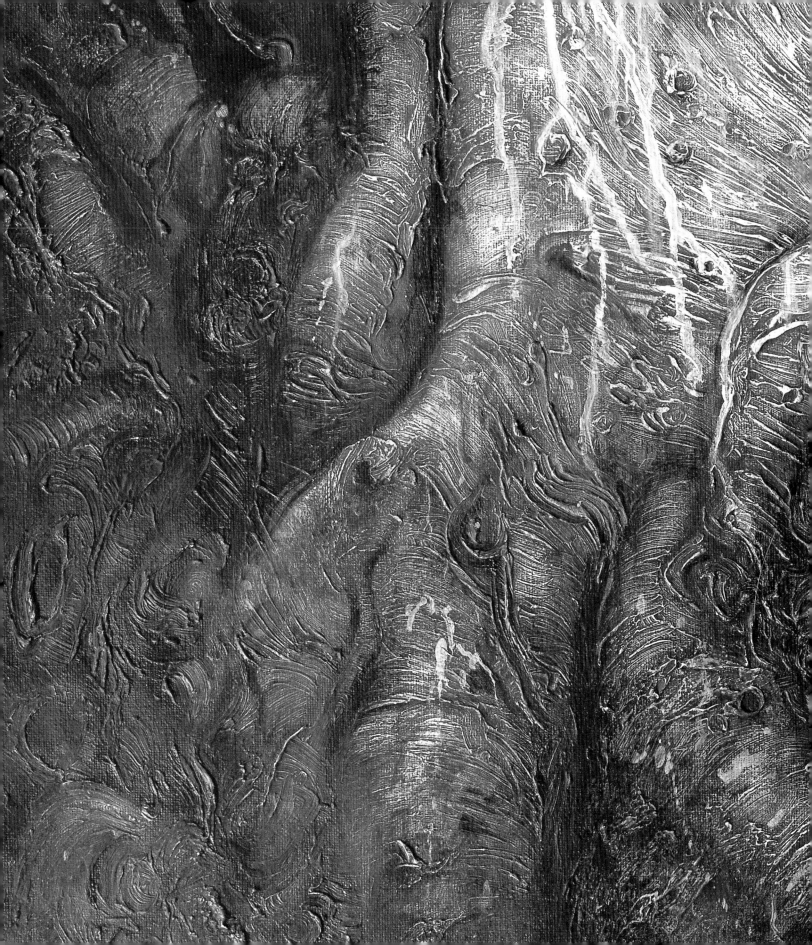

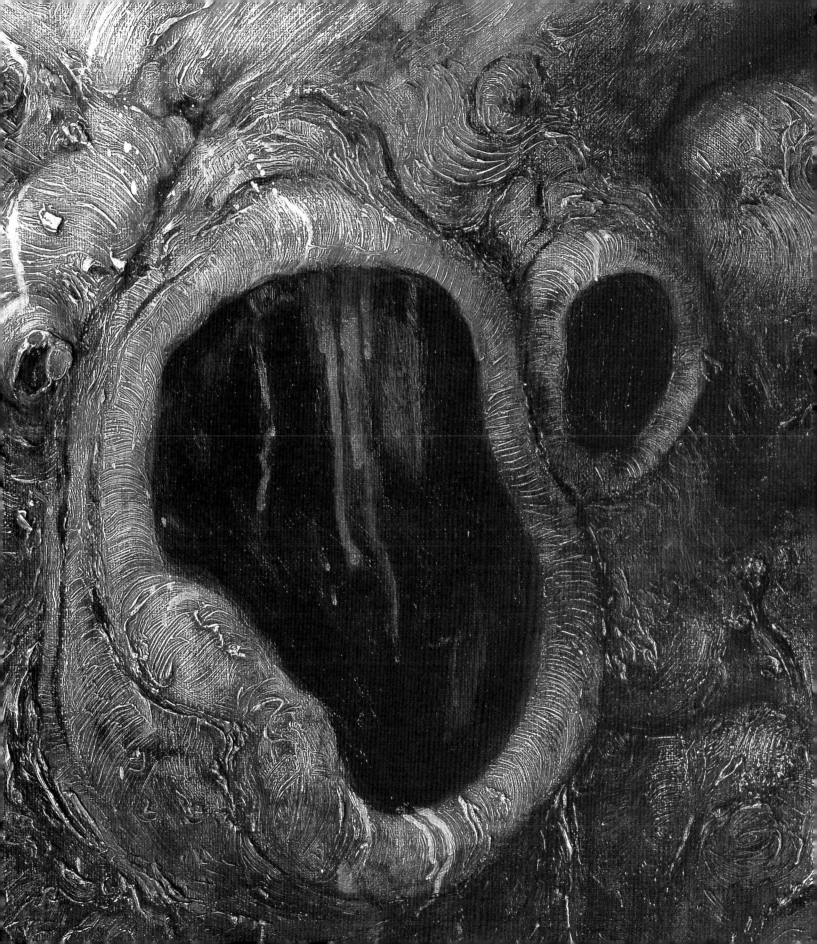

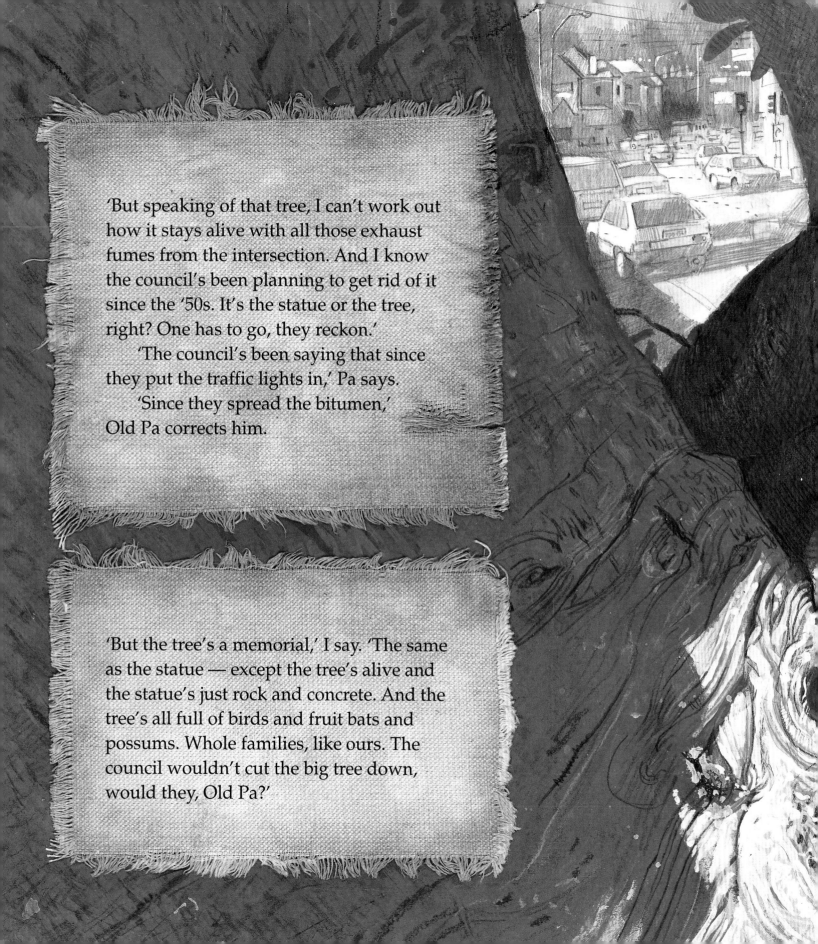

'But speaking of that tree, I can't work out how it stays alive with all those exhaust fumes from the intersection. And I know the council's been planning to get rid of it since the '50s. It's the statue or the tree, right? One has to go, they reckon.'

'The council's been saying that since they put the traffic lights in,' Pa says.

'Since they spread the bitumen,' Old Pa corrects him.

'But the tree's a memorial,' I say. 'The same as the statue — except the tree's alive and the statue's just rock and concrete. And the tree's all full of birds and fruit bats and possums. Whole families, like ours. The council wouldn't cut the big tree down, would they, Old Pa?'

'It's a traffic hazard, they say.'

'It's lifting the bitumen, they say.'

'It drops seeds on cars, they say.'

'It obscures the traffic lights, they say.'

'It's knocking the statue over, they say.'

'Then I'll fight the council,' I say. 'Because the tree's a memorial too. They have to see that. A living memorial ...'

But Old Pa laughs. 'They'll beat you, son,' he says. 'The big boys will beat you every time. They'll chop you to bits ...'

Then he smiles and says, 'Still, that don't mean they'll forget you. It's the fight in you they'll remember. That memory won't die — not like my old bones. Even concrete and rock won't last forever. But memories, now they're different. Memories, they're ever-livin' things. Like you say, son, like our tree …'

And now that I think about it,
I know what he said is true.

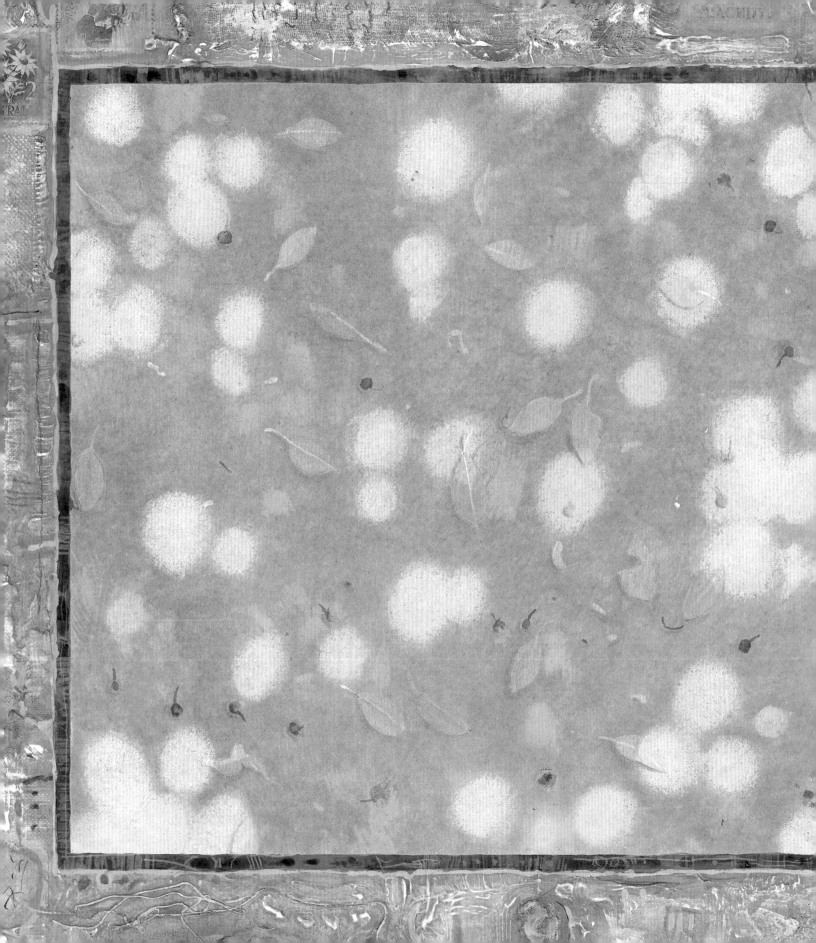